## Foreword

**By Marty Brennaman**

As baseball's oldest professional franchise, the Cincinnati Reds have a history and tradition that is unmatched by any other team in our grand game. Since joining the Reds on Radio broadcast booth in 1974, I have witnessed first-hand many of the team's historic moments. During that time, I have also had a chance to see just how much Reds baseball means to all the team's fans throughout Reds Country.

With this book, author Joel Altman has presented this rich tradition in a fun way that helps bring the history of Reds baseball to a whole new generation of Reds fans. Just as Mr. Redlegs comes away with many stories to tell of his adventures through Reds history, fans through the years have told their own stories of special memories and experiences at Reds games, passing down the passion for Reds baseball that makes us all feel like kids again every time we enter the ballpark.

**For Milton, Albert, Baby Megan, the people and families of Reds Country and all Reds fans past, present and future.**

**Special Thanks:**
**This book would not have been possible without Karen Forgus, whose support took it from a simple idea to a reality. I would also like to thank Michael Anderson, the staff of the Reds Hall of Fame and Museum, Lori Watt, Ralph Mitchell, PNC Bank, Marty Brennaman and my wife Ashley.**

*Mr. Redlegs and His Great Adventure: A Journey through Cincinnati Reds History*



PRT0812A

Printed in the United States

Library of Congress Control Number: 2012934077

ISBN-13: 9781937406363
ISBN-10: 1937406369

www.mascotbooks.com

# Mr. Redlegs and His Great Adventure

**By Joel Altman**

**With Foreword by
Marty Brennaman**

**Illustrated by Tim Williams**

It was a beautiful day in Cincinnati, and Mr. Redlegs was looking forward to the baseball game at Great American Ball Park later in the evening. He had some extra time, so he decided to go to his favorite place: the Reds Hall of Fame and Museum located right next door!

GREAT AMERICAN BALL PARK

Inside the Kids Clubhouse of the museum, Mr. Redlegs found a room filled with old-fashioned baseball equipment. Curious, he picked up an old-fashioned baseball cap. As he placed the hat on his head, something strange happened…

…Mr. Redlegs was instantly transported back in time! As he looked around in shock, he recognized Union Grounds from old photographs in the Reds Museum. It must be 1869, the year the Cincinnati Red Stockings became baseball's first professional team!

Mr. Redlegs adjusted the hat, and suddenly a horse-drawn carriage swept him up and took him two miles north to the Avenue Grounds. After another wild ride he was ejected at the corner of Findlay St. and Western Ave., which in 1902 was the home of the ballpark known as the Palace of the Fans.

In 1911, Mr. Redlegs watched as the Palace of the Fans was demolished and in its place a new ballpark, Redland Field, opened in 1912. He then watched the excitement on the field as the Redlegs, led by Hall of Famer Edd Roush, defeated the White Sox in the 1919 World Series!

Mr. Redlegs adjusted the hat again, and was suddenly sitting in the stands as Redland Field became known as Crosley Field. It was 1935 and Mr. Redlegs felt the charge in the crisp evening air as the Reds defeated the Phillies in the first-ever night game in Major League history!

Then Mr. Redlegs stood in awe as he watched Johnny Vander Meer become the only pitcher in Major League history to throw back-to-back no-hitters on June 11th and 15th, 1938!

Mr. Redlegs was whisked through the 1939 season. The Reds, led by Hall of Fame catcher Ernie Lombardi, emerged as National League champions. However, the Reds fell to the New York Yankees in the World Series that year. His sadness was soon lifted in the 1940 season when the Reds became World Champions for the first time in 21 years by defeating the Detroit Tigers in the World Series!

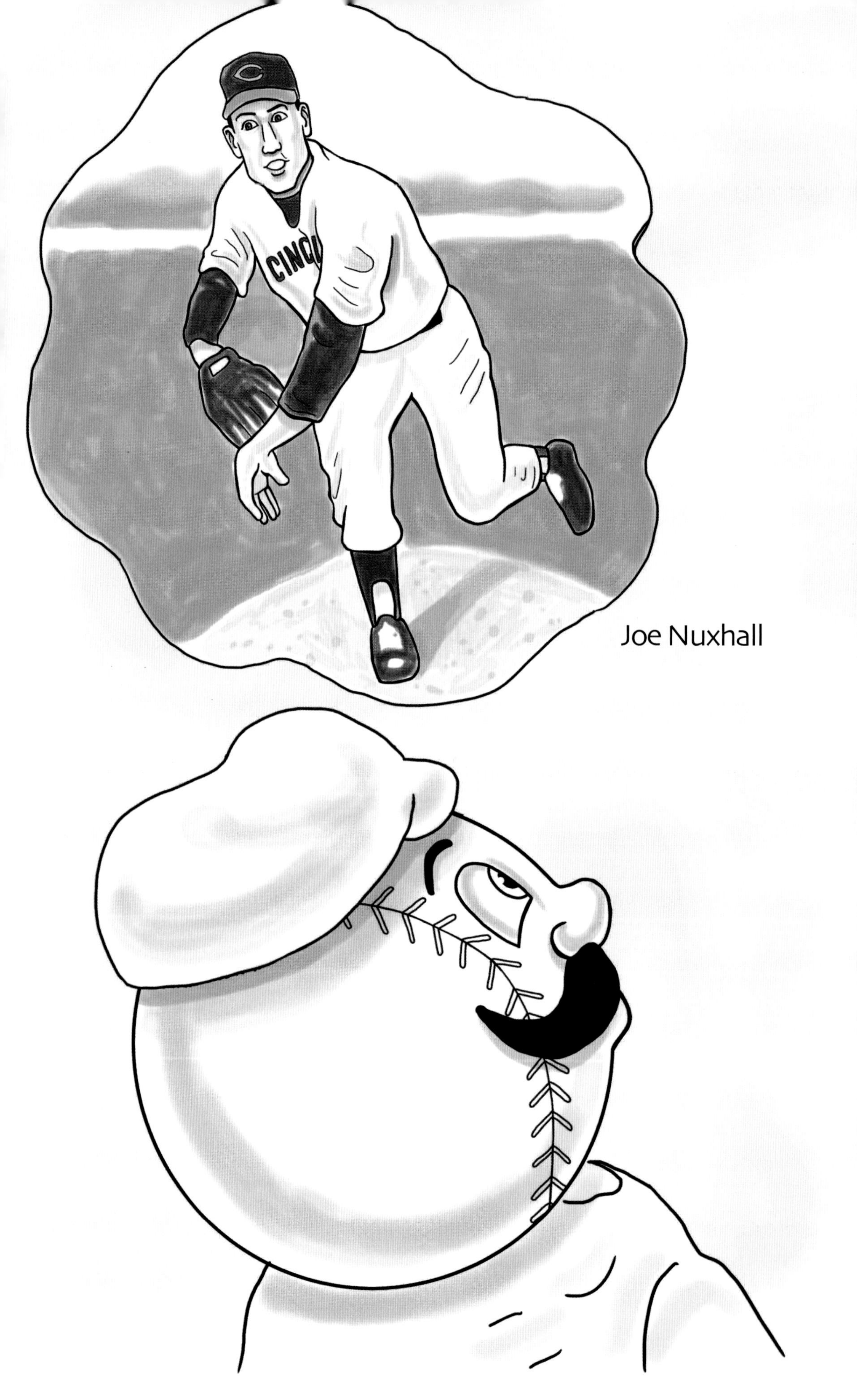

Joe Nuxhall

Ted Kluszewski

Frank Robinson

As Mr. Redlegs sped through time, he recognized more famous faces from Reds history. He watched from the stands on June 10, 1944 when 15-year-old Hamilton, Ohio native, Joe Nuxhall, pitched for the Reds. He would later become known around town as "The Ol' Left-Hander" and would broadcast Reds games on the radio with his good friend and Radio Hall of Famer, Marty Brennaman. Mr. Redlegs saw Ted Kluszewski become the National League home run leader in 1954 and Frank Robinson become the 1956 National League Rookie of the Year.

Suddenly, Mr. Redlegs came to a stop on the banks of the Ohio River, right in front of the brand new Riverfront Stadium. Mr. Redlegs knew it was 1970 and with the new stadium and management, things were about to get exciting! As he looked on, new manager George "Sparky" Anderson led the Reds to the World Series battling the Baltimore Orioles. Even though the Reds lost the World Series that year, Mr. Redlegs knew that The Big Red Machine was starting to form and another exciting era in Reds history was about to begin!

George
"Sparky"
Anderson

Pete Rose
Joe
Morgan

Tony Perez

Johnny Bench

Mr. Redlegs continued to watch the Reds as Joe Morgan, Pete Rose, Tony Perez and Johnny Bench led the Reds to the World Series again in 1972. After beating the Pittsburgh Pirates in 5 games to win the pennant the Reds lost to the Oakland A's in the 7th game of the World Series. But, Mr. Redlegs knew that with this core group of players and an excellent pitching staff, the Reds would soon prove to be unbeatable!

Mr. Redlegs moved forward in time as the Reds headed into the 1975 season and World Series. He watched one of the most exciting games in World Series history.

It went late into the night as the Reds and the Boston Red Sox battled back and forth during Game 6 until the Red Sox won in the 12th inning. However, the Reds became World Champions once again after defeating the Red Sox in Game 7! With The Big Red Machine, the Reds had a team that was in perfect working order. Mr. Redlegs was breathless as he watched the most exciting team in baseball history take the field.

Mr. Redlegs was now in the year 1976 and watched The Big Red Machine dominate their opponents. To his delight, the Reds emerged victorious again in 1976. Mr. Redlegs jumped with excitement as the Reds swept the Yankees, to be crowned World Series Champions for the second season in a row!

This is a feat which has not been accomplished by a National League team since! Mr. Redlegs waved the old hat and cheered as he watched Joe Morgan win the National League MVP in 1975 and 1976! "Way to go, Little Joe!" yelled Mr. Redlegs.

George Foster

As Mr. Redlegs moved into the late 1970s, The Big Red Machine era was winding down as some members left the team. But there were still many exciting moments to come. Mr. Redlegs was beyond impressed when he saw George Foster become the 1977 National League MVP and hit 52 home runs that year. Now that's a lot of dingers! Mr. Redlegs threw his hands in the air and applauded as he watched Pete Rose's 44-game hitting streak along with Tom Seaver's no hitter at Riverfront Stadium in 1978.

Tom Seaver

Pete Rose

As the hands of his watch continued to spin, Mr. Redlegs watched Johnny Bench round the bases as he hit his final home run on "Johnny Bench Night", September 17, 1983. Bench, the greatest catcher of all time, is one of Mr. Redlegs' heroes.

He watched in awe as Pete Rose returned to the Reds in 1984 and broke Ty Cobb's all-time hit record on September 11, 1985. Rose hit a single into left-center field for hit number 4192, becoming baseball's all-time "Hit King!" What an exciting moment in Reds history! Three years later, Mr. Redlegs watched Tom Browning's perfect game on September 16, 1988 – the only perfect game in Reds history. Chris Sabo became the National League Rookie of the Year in 1988 and Mr. Redlegs watched the All-Star Game played at Riverfront Stadium for the second and final time.

Jose Rijo

Mr. Redlegs touched the brim of the old hat and was instantly transported to 1990. He saw the Reds go "wire to wire," which means they started the year in first place and stayed there the entire season, sweeping the Oakland A's for another World Series title!

Mr. Redlegs was amazed at the "Nasty Boys" relief pitchers: Norm Charlton, Randy Myers, and Rob Dibble. They helped manager "Sweet" Lou Piniella lead the team to victory during one of the most exciting seasons ever!

Mr. Redlegs continued forward in time and cheered as Barry Larkin was crowned the 1995 National League MVP and became the first shortstop to hit 30 home runs and steal 30 bases in one season in 1996!

He rejoiced when Ken Griffey, Jr. came to the Reds in 2000 to play for his hometown team and wore his father's number 30 on his jersey. He watched in silence with a tear in his eye as fans said goodbye to the old Riverfront Stadium in 2002. Mr. Redlegs was soon elated to see his new home, Great American Ball Park, open in 2003!

Mr. Redlegs knew he was almost home, so he held the hat tight to his head as he saw the Reds make the playoffs in 2010. He thought his heart might burst as he witnessed Jay Bruce's walk-off home run to clinch the National League Central Division. He ducked as Aroldis "the Cuban Missile" Chapman threw the fastest pitch ever recorded – 105.1 miles per hour! Now that is fast!

He then saw Joey Votto become the 2010 National League MVP and lead the team into the future. What an exciting time for Reds fans!

Clutching the hat, Mr. Redlegs was finally transported back to the present-day Reds Hall of Fame. He thought about all the things he'd seen that day. He looked around the beautiful Hall of Fame, filled with treasures commemorating all the wonderful events and players he'd just had the honor to witness firsthand. Mr. Redlegs' mascot friends, Rosie Red, Gapper, and Mr. Red were looking for him. He told them about his amazing adventure. They all hoped to have exciting adventures in Reds history, too!

Mr. Redlegs knew there would be more wonderful moments in the years to come!

From the Findlay Market Parade and Opening Day, to the All-Star Game, and into October, the Reds are a team that continues to be rich in history and tradition.

As Mr. Redlegs returned the old cap to the Kids Clubhouse, he glanced back for a moment. He couldn't quite believe all the amazing events he'd seen that day. Then, with a huge smile, he quietly shut the door and got ready to head back to the ballpark. Mr. Redlegs and his friends couldn't wait to watch more Cincinnati Reds history in the making!

- 1867-1870: The Union Grounds was the home of the Red Stockings and the grandstand was known as "Grand Duchess."
- 1869-1870: The Red Stockings won 81 games in a row.
- 1876-1879: The Avenue Grounds was the home of the Red Stockings.
- 1938-1940: The National League MVPs were all Reds players; Ernie Lombardi, Bucky Walters, and Frank McCormick.
- 1950's: Ted Kluszewski's arms were so big that he had to cut the sleeves off his uniform to be able to swing his bat!
- 1970: Riverfront Stadium opens. It had an all artificial playing surface with only dirt around the bases, home plate and the pitcher's mound.
- 1970, 1972: Johnny Bench is named the National League MVP in both seasons.
- 1975: The Reds won a club record 108 regular season games and defeated the Boston Red Sox in the World Series. Pete Rose was named World Series MVP.
- 1976: During the postseason, the Reds went undefeated by sweeping the Phillies and the Yankees to become back-to-back World Champions. Johnny Bench was named World Series MVP.

- 1978: Pete Rose hit safely in 44 consecutive games; a record for the National League. Only Joe DiMaggio has hit in more consecutive games with a record of 56.
- Pitcher Mario Soto holds the Reds record for most Opening Day starts with 6. 1982-1986, 1988.
- 1990: Jose Rijo was named the World Series MVP with two wins. Outfielder Billy Hatcher set a World Series record with 7 consecutive hits and a .750 batting average that beat a record previously held by Babe Ruth.
- 2003: Great American Ball Park opened.
- 2004: The Reds Hall of Fame and Museum opened right next to the Great American Ball Park.
- 2010: The Reds spring training moved from Florida to the new complex in Goodyear, Arizona.
- 2012: Barry Larkin, who spent his entire career with the Reds from 1986 to 2004, was elected to the Baseball Hall of Fame.
- Mr. Redlegs has three mascot friends; Rosie Red, Gapper, and the new Mr. Red. All four of them enjoy meeting fans and hanging out in the Fan Zone at Great American Ball Park. So come by and say hello!

**Cincinnati Reds Retired Numbers:**

| 1 | 5 | 8 | 10 | 13 | 18 | 20 | 24 |
|---|---|---|---|---|---|---|---|

#1 - Fred Hutchinson, #5 - Johnny Bench, #8 - Joe Morgan, #10 - Sparky Anderson, #13 - Dave Concepción, #18 - Ted Kluszewski, #20 - Frank Robinson, #24 - Tony Perez

* #11 Barry Larkin in 2012

**"...rounding third and heading for home."**

**-Joe Nuxhall,**
**"The Ol' Left-Hander"**

REDS
TM